MR.
NONSENSE

by Roger Hargreaves

Mr Nonsense had no sense at all.

Not a scrap.

I mean, he lived in a tree.

A tree!

Can you imagine?

"Why do you live in a tree?" Mr Happy asked him one day.

"Because," replied Mr Nonsense, "I tried living on the ground, but that was too high up, so I moved to a tree to be nearer the ground."

"What nonsense," snorted Mr Happy.

"Thank you," replied Mr Nonsense.

And, do you know what Mr Nonsense liked to eat?

Porridge!

Nothing wrong with that you might say.

But, porridge on toast!

Really!

"Why do you like porridge on toast?" Mr Nosey asked him one day.

"Because," replied Mr Nonsense, "I tried porridge sandwiches and I didn't like them!"

And, do you know where Mr Nonsense sleeps every night?

In a rowing boat!

In his bedroom.

In his house.

Up a tree.

"Why do you sleep in a rowing boat?" Mr Strong asked him one day.

"Because," replied Mr Nonsense, "I tried sleeping in a motor boat but it was somewhat uncomfortable!"

Mr Nonsense lives, as you might very well expect, in a country called Nonsenseland.

Now, I know somebody else who lives in Nonsenseland.

Do you?

That's right.

Mr Silly!

Mr Silly and Mr Nonsense were close friends and saw a lot of each other.

Mr Nonsense was often round at Mr Silly's house playing jigsaw puzzles.

They used to throw the pieces at each other!

How silly!

And Mr Silly was often round at Mr Nonsense's house playing cards.

They used to tear them up to see who could get the most pieces out of one card!

What nonsense!

However, this story is about the time it snowed in Nonsenseland.

It didn't very often snow, but one winter it did.

Now, tell me, what colour is snow?

No, in Nonsenseland, when it snows, it doesn't snow white snow.

It snows yellow snow!

Don't ask me why.

But it does.

Yellow snow!

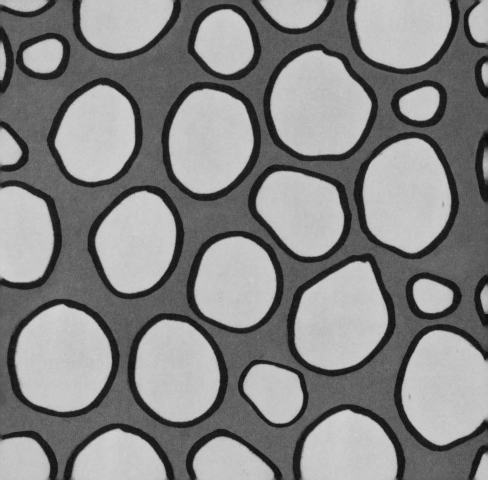

And, when Mr Silly woke up one morning, the whole of Nonsenseland was covered.

"I say," he said when he looked out of his bedroom window. "Snow!"

And he was so excited he rushed round to Mr Nonsense's house.

Mr Nonsense was asleep.

In his boat.

"Wake up!" cried Mr Silly. "Wake up, and come and look out of the window."

"What ever on earth is it?" grumbled Mr Nonsense, rubbing the sleep out of his eyes as he got up and went across to his bedroom window.

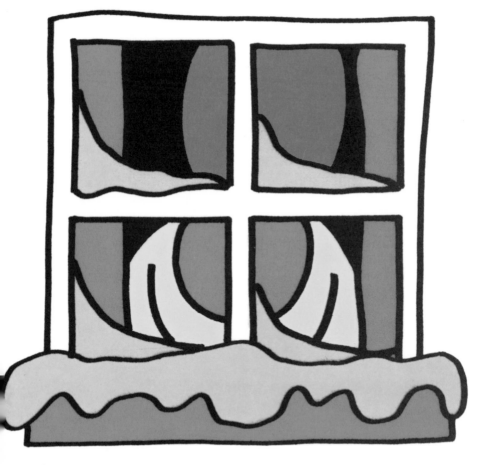

"I say," he said, looking out. "Custard!"

"That isn't custard, you silly banana," cried Mr Silly. "That's snow!"

He rushed downstairs.

"Come on," he called.

And that day, Mr Silly and Mr Nonsense had one of the very best days of their lives.

They had a snowball fight.

Mr Silly's snowballs were round.

Mr Nonsense made snowballs that somehow or other came out sort of square!

They built a snowman.

A very silly nonsensical sort of a snowman.

"Come on," said Mr Nonsense that afternoon. "Let's go tobogganing!"

"But we don't have a toboggan," said Mr Silly.

"Oh no, we don't," agreed Mr Nonsense.

Mr Silly thought.

"Oh yes, we do," he cried.

And Mr Silly ran back to Mr Nonsense's house, and came back with his bed.

"Wheeeee!" they shouted together as they slid faster and faster down the hill in their rowing boat toboggan.

It was a wonderful day.

And that evening, after having supper together (porridge pie), Mr Nonsense suggested that they played a game.

"What shall we play?" asked Mr Silly.

"Draughts," suggested Mr Nonsense.

"I've forgotten how to play draughts," said Mr Silly.

"Oh, it's easy," replied Mr Nonsense.

And went round and opened all the doors and windows!

"There we are," he said. "Draughts!"

What nonsense!

3 Great Offers for MR.MEN Fans!

MR.MEN TOKEN

1 New Mr. Men or Little Miss Library Bus Presentation Cases

A brand new stronger, roomier school bus library box, with sturdy carrying handle and stay-closed fasteners.

The full colour, wipe-clean boxes make a great home for your full collection.

They're just £5.99 inc P&P and free bookmark!

☐ MR. MEN ☐ LITTLE MISS (please tick and order overleaf)

2 Door Hangers and Posters

In every Mr. Men and Little Miss book like this one, you will find a special token. Collect 6 tokens and we will send you a brilliant Mr. Men or Little Miss poster and a Mr. Men or Little Miss double sided full colour bedroom door hanger of your choice. Simply tick your choice in the list and tape a 50p coin for your two items to this page.

PLEASE STICK YOUR 50P COIN HERE

Door Hangers (please tick)
☐ Mr. Nosey & Mr. Muddle
☐ Mr. Slow & Mr. Busy
☐ Mr. Messy & Mr. Quiet
☐ Mr. Perfect & Mr. Forgetful
☐ Little Miss Fun & Little Miss Late
☐ Little Miss Helpful & Little Miss Tidy
☐ Little Miss Busy & Little Miss Brainy
☐ Little Miss Star & Little Miss Fun

Posters (please tick)
☐ MR.MEN
☐ LITTLE MISS

3 Sixteen Beautiful Fridge Magnets – any 2 for £2.00! inc.P&P

They're very special collector's items!
Simply tick your first and second* choices from the list below
of any 2 characters!

1st Choice
- ☐ Mr. Happy
- ☐ Mr. Lazy
- ☐ Mr. Topsy-Turvy
- ☐ Mr. Bounce
- ☐ Mr. Bump
- ☐ Mr. Small
- ☐ Mr. Snow
- ☐ Mr. Wrong

- ☐ Mr. Daydream
- ☐ Mr. Tickle
- ☐ Mr. Greedy
- ☐ Mr. Funny
- ☐ Little Miss Giggles
- ☐ Little Miss Splendid
- ☐ Little Miss Naughty
- ☐ Little Miss Sunshine

2nd Choice
- ☐ Mr. Happy
- ☐ Mr. Lazy
- ☐ Mr. Topsy-Turvy
- ☐ Mr. Bounce
- ☐ Mr. Bump
- ☐ Mr. Small
- ☐ Mr. Snow
- ☐ Mr. Wrong

- ☐ Mr. Daydream
- ☐ Mr. Tickle
- ☐ Mr. Greedy
- ☐ Mr. Funny
- ☐ Little Miss Giggles
- ☐ Little Miss Splendid
- ☐ Little Miss Naughty
- ☐ Little Miss Sunshine

*Only in case your first choice is out of stock.

CUT ALONG DOTTED LINE AND RETURN THIS WHOLE PAGE

— TO BE COMPLETED BY AN ADULT —

**To apply for any of these great offers, ask an adult to complete the coupon below and send it with
the appropriate payment and tokens, if needed, to MR. MEN OFFERS, PO BOX 7, MANCHESTER M19 2HD**

☐ Please send ____ Mr. Men Library case(s) and/or ____ Little Miss Library case(s) at £5.99 each inc P&P

☐ Please send a poster and door hanger as selected overleaf. I enclose six tokens plus a 50p coin for P&P

☐ Please send me ____ pair(s) of Mr. Men/Little Miss fridge magnets, as selected above at £2.00 inc P&P

Fan's Name _____

Address _____

_____ **Postcode** _____

Date of Birth _____

Name of Parent/Guardian _____

Total amount enclosed £_____

☐ **I enclose a cheque/postal order payable to Egmont Books Limited**

☐ **Please charge my MasterCard/Visa/Amex/Switch or Delta account** (delete as appropriate)

Card Number

Expiry date __/__ Signature _____

Please allow 28 days for delivery. We reserve the right to change the terms of this offer at any time
but we offer a 14 day money back guarantee. This does not affect your statutory rights.

MR.MEN LITTLE MISS
Mr. Men and Little Miss™ & ©Mrs. Roger Hargreaves